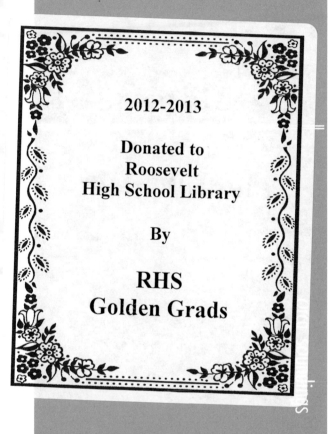

ORCA BOOK PUBLISHERS

HIGH SCHOOL

SEATTLE, WASHINGTON

National Library of Canada Cataloguing in Publication Data

Withers, Pam
Breathless / Pam Withers.

(Orca soundings)
ISBN 1-55143-480-6

I. Title. II. Series.

PS8595.I8453B74 2005   jC813'.6   C2005-904466-7

First published in the United States, 2005
Library of Congress Control Number: 2005930531

Summary: Beverly gets into serious trouble when
her starvation diet interferes with her scuba diving.

Orca Book Publishers gratefully acknowledges the support for its publishing
programs provided by the following agencies: the Government of Canada
through the Book Publishing Industry Development Program (BPIDP), the
Canada Council for the Arts, and the British Columbia Arts Council.

Cover design: Lynn O'Rourke
Cover photography: Firstlight.ca

Orca Book Publishers
P.O Box 5626, Stn. B
Victoria, BC Canada
v8r 6s4

Orca Book Publishers
PO Box 468
Custer, WA USA
98240-0468

www.orcabook.com
Printed and bound in Canada
Printed on 50% post-consumer recycled paper,
processed chlorine free using vegetable, low VOC inks.

08 07 06 05 • 4 3 2 1

Dedicated to my dive buddy,
Shannon Young.

With special thanks to our instructor,
Darren Moss, to B.C. Dive and Kayak
and to Kathy Guild.

Chapter One

I was okay until that toothy moray eel appeared. It came out of nowhere in the murky water and veered straight at me—honest. It was like it wanted a head-on collision with my mask.

Now, I'm not a girl easily scared by a fish. But here's the deal about scuba diving: The water magnifies objects one-third larger than they really are. So it seemed like some giant mutant was attacking me. Besides, I learned scuba diving in the lakes around Winnipeg, where I live. And this was only my second day of visiting my uncle in Kauai, Hawaii, over Christmas break. So I didn't know that I was supposed to wear more weights on my weight belt. As it turns out, tropical water floats you higher than the cold stuff in Manitoba lakes. Even if you're a fat, ugly fifteen-year-old like me, it floats you higher.

Okay, so I'm not fat. I'm pudgy. And I'm not as ugly as that freaky fish was, for sure. It scared me. I'd already been struggling with staying close by my uncle, thanks to having too many weights on. So I lifted my hand to scare away the eel, and that accidentally tore the regulator out of my mouth. The regulator is the mouthpiece that connects to your oxygen tank. It lets you breathe.

Knocking the regulator out of my mouth made me swallow a little water, which made me panic. And the thing about panicking when you're forty feet under the ocean's surface is that you can drown, and you know you can drown. In fact, you can't breathe without your regulator even if you're not panicking.

You're also not supposed to hold your breath, because there's pressure underwater. That means if you're not breathing out bubbles while the regulator is out, your chest might expand until it explodes. Not really. But something like that. I finished my scuba diver certification a year ago, but I can't remember everything.

So I was exhaling. But before I got the regulator back in, I was flailing around, and my arm—the one trying to scare the eel away—was all tangled in my regulator hose. And I swallowed some water before I got the regulator back into my mouth. That made me feel sick. So now I was sick to my stomach *and* full-on scared. Now, I don't want to get gross and all, but here's the truth: If you throw up when you're forty feet underwater and trying to breathe on a regulator, it's okay. Honest! Scuba diver gear is made to take that. Can you believe it? I mean, it lets you keep breathing in between upchucking. Otherwise I wouldn't still be around.

So I was breathing and barfing and crying and kicking around, certain I was going to die. But my Uncle Tom, who's my favorite uncle, was great. He swam right in front of me and locked his reassuring blue eyes on mine. He made sign language to tell me to breathe slowly. And he rested his hands on my shoulders. It worked. Just knowing he was there. Him being a scuba diving instructor and all. He owns his own dive shop, runs diving trips and stuff. That's why I was in Kauai over Christmas, because one of his two employees had quit. He knew he couldn't replace the guy until January. He knew I loved diving and figured I could help out during my break. So he paid my airfare all the way from Winnipeg. Pretty nice, I say.

I was glad he was with me when I was panicking. If I was going to drown, it might as well be with him beside me, being nice to me. But like I said, the regulator kept me breathing until I was finished being sick. And then, kicking his flippers, he steered us up to the surface. Nice and slowly. If you don't do things right in scuba diving, bad stuff can happen.

The shop assistant who still works for Uncle Tom found that out the hard way.

Her name is Weniki. That's Hawaiian for "Wendy." She's deaf because of a diving accident. It was a couple of years ago. Now she just rinses diving gear in the shop. Or fills tanks and does stuff on the computer for him. But she's not very friendly. She has hardly said a word to me since I got to Kauai. It's not because she's deaf. She can talk if she wants to. Even though she hardly ever does, to anyone. She's just a sour old middle-aged lady who doesn't like kids. At least, that's what I think. So I mostly ignore her.

Anyway, Uncle Tom got me to the surface without me drowning.

"Beverly, you're okay. Take some deep breaths. I'm right here."

"I'm sorry, Uncle Tom," I said, lowering my mask and trying not to cry.

He hesitated. I could see he was surprised I'd panicked and was disappointed in me. But he was trying to be nice. "You swallowed a bit of water?"

"Yeah, I guess."

"More than you could handle. But you did get the regulator back in. I didn't have to help you there, Beverly." That must've been the only positive thing he could think of to say. He really was trying to be nice.

"Good thing."

He frowned. "Guess we shouldn't have gone so deep on our first dive together. My fault."

"No. My fault. I shouldn't panic so easily. I'm really sorry. I promise it won't happen again."

He nodded and patted my shoulder. I could tell he didn't believe me. "Rest here as long as you like, Beverly. Then we can head to shore." The two of us were hanging in the water beside our little dive buoy. "Unless you want to dive some more."

He had to be joking. I hoped he was joking. I didn't answer, and I couldn't look at him. I felt ashamed. Would he let me dive again after this?

"Beverly," he said after a minute, "I think you might benefit from a refresher course in a swimming pool before we go diving again."

I hung my head and nodded a little.

"I know you're a good diver. Your dad tells me you're a good diver. But I think it wouldn't hurt to do a refresher course. Just to boost your confidence. Okay with you?"

Confidence. Not my best quality, for sure. I'd failed today. He had no confidence in me. I nodded my head again.

Uncle Tom slapped me gently on my back, gave me a beaming smile, and we set off for the beach. The beach with all the bikinied girls and their dark tans. I sighed. Even if I hadn't just stepped off a plane from Winnipeg, my skin as white as the ice on our lakes, I'd look like a fish out of water lying next to them. Or rather, like a beached, blubbery whale.

I hate skinny girls. I've never been one. And I hate how they always get asked out. Just before I left Winnipeg for the holiday break, my best friend was the only one besides me in our crowd who wasn't going out with anyone. In other words, all our other friends were never around anymore for good times. Then she got asked out for the December Dance. So guess who's the last one standing now.

But I got lucky. I didn't have to go to the December Dance because Uncle Tom invited me to Kauai instead.

As I sat on the airplane, I made myself two promises. During this break, I'd lose ten pounds if it killed me. And sometime soon, I'd get myself a boyfriend, whatever it took.

Dumb? Of course. But who cares? That's what I decided to do—assuming, that is, that I don't accidentally drown first. Which I did not today, thanks to Uncle Tom.

Chapter Two

The pool was close enough to walk to from Uncle Tom's apartment above the dive shop. Uncle Tom didn't seem to mind when I "slept" through breakfast. Really, of course, I was reading in my room. I pretended I was sleeping in so he wouldn't notice me not eating breakfast before I headed out.

He rapped softly. "Morning, Beverly." I love how he always uses my full name, never "Bev."

"Hi, Uncle Tom. Just getting up," I called out.

"Good girl. I've left you some pancakes and sausages. Abe's expecting you at nine. He's a good instructor. See you at noon downstairs, then."

"You bet." I felt a little guilty not eating with him. But I was eating as little as I could. At this rate, I reckoned I'd be in a bikini in no time.

I got up, dressed and wandered into the kitchen. I leaned over the pan of warm pancakes and sausages. I directed the seriously delicious smell up through my nostrils. Hey, smelling is free. There are no calories in smelling. Then I walked the plate over to the sink and fed it all down the garbage disposal unit.

Fifteen minutes later, I approached the local indoor pool. Since I was five minutes early, I sat down on a low wall across the street and sniffed some tropical blossoms hanging over my shoulder. Beverly, I told myself, this sure isn't Winnipeg in December. A gorgeous guy, maybe eighteen, was leaning against the pool building, watching people pass by. His eyes would follow anything female until she was out of sight.

He leapt to open the doors for two girls exiting the pool behind him.

"Allow me," I heard him say. "By the way, I'm a talent scout for *Baywatch*. Care to leave your phone numbers with me?"

The girls erupted into laughter and scurried down the steps, leaving Sir Gallivant grinning. I headed across the street. He never even glanced at me until I tripped on the stairs.

"Hey kid, you all right?" he asked.

"Fine," I declared, my face hot.

"Sure now?" His eyes were already fastened on someone who'd appeared up the street.

As I pried open the heavy door, a stifling humidity and chlorine smell greeted me. A man in swim trunks was carrying dive tanks to the pool's edge. He looked up.

"Beverly McLeod?"

I nodded. He was Uncle Tom's age, around thirty.

"I'm Abe. Ready for your private lesson?"

"Yes." At least he hadn't said "refresher course for flunkies."

He smiled and nodded toward the ladies' changing room. "Go ahead and change. I have your tanks ready. The divemaster will be here soon."

A divemaster, I knew, was an experienced helper. When I emerged, someone was arranging tanks and masks beside Abe. I noted a muscular back and a head of dark, curly hair. When he turned, I blushed. It was Sir Gallivant.

"Beverly, this is Garth Olsen, the divemaster. Garth, this is Beverly McLeod."

"Pleased to meet you," Garth said, cracking a grin.

"Uh, hi."

"Beverly is Tom McLeod's niece," Abe informed Garth.

"Really?" Garth, eyes widening, studied me more carefully. "Love your uncle's shop. How come we haven't seen you around before?"

"She's visiting from Winnipeg, Canada," Abe said as he reached for his weight belt. Did he think I couldn't speak for myself?

"Winnipeg!" Garth exclaimed. "They call that *Winter*-peg, don't they? Must be a short diving season up there."

"Actually, people dive year-round," I said, hating the defensive tone that crept into my voice. "Some people cut holes in the ice and dive midwinter." Not that *I* had.

"You don't say," Garth said, hands on his hips. He was looking me up and down now, way too slowly, eyes gleaming. "That sounds hard-core."

"So," Abe interrupted, "Beverly, as soon as you've got your gear on, I'll watch you and Garth do buddy checks on one another." That meant we'd inspect each other to make sure we had all our stuff on and buckled or hooked up correctly. "Then I'll have you demonstrate a deep-water entry, a snorkel/regulator exchange under the surface and the five-step descent."

Easy stuff. Scuba diving kindergarten. "Okay," I said.

"Then we'll practice underwater signals, breathing from an alternate air source and flooding and clearing your mask underwater."

I looked at Garth. He oozed confidence. It reassured me. "And removing your weight belt underwater."

One by one, I tackled the skills Abe demanded. Only once did I have to burst to the surface in a fit of nervousness. Abe patiently reviewed things, and Garth's eye contact and nods helped me through the exercises.

Once, when Garth and I surfaced before Abe, I said, "You're a good divemaster."

"The best!" he responded with a wink. "And totally available to work for your uncle anytime."

I blinked. Oh, so I was the niece who could get him a job, was I? Mr. Full-of-Himself.

"Excellent session, Beverly," Abe said as we rinsed our gear. "You're all systems go for whatever dives Tom wants to take you on. I'm sure you'll enjoy our tropical waters." His smile was kind. "Welcome to Hawaii."

"Thanks," I said, reaching to lift my tank, only to find it snatched away by Garth's muscular arm.

"Relax. You're the customer," he said. "Way to go, Miss Winnipeg. See you around." His gait quickened as a bikinied girl stepped out of the changing room and floated gracefully along the deck ahead of him.

Chapter Three

I flew up the back steps of Uncle Tom's shop, excited to tell him that I'd passed. I nearly slammed into Weniki. She was carrying a plastic tub of wet suits to the big sink outside the back entrance. That's where she spends most of her day, rinsing and hanging.

Her eyebrows slanted in disapproval at my rush.

"I passed!" I told her. I said it while looking straight at her, so she could read my lips.

She shrugged and set her bin down. Then she reached for her plastic apron. All she cares about is work, I thought. Who cares if she isn't impressed with me passing? I smoothed my T-shirt over my shorts, which were feeling looser around my waist already. Amazing what three days of almost no eating will do.

"Beverly! You're back. How'd it go?" asked my uncle as he delivered another tub to Weniki.

"I passed! No problems!" I said.

"Excellent, my dear. I thought you would. Isn't that great, Weniki?" He was careful to let her read his lips, even though he knew some sign language. Weniki gave him a cursory smile and nod. "Well now, Weniki," he continued to address her, "take a break for lunch. I just bought some food next door."

Next door would be the delicatessen. The three of us filed into the staff room. Uncle Tom pushed the tray of food toward me. Weniki started reading a diving magazine in between bites of her sandwich.

"So, Beverly," Uncle Tom said as I popped grapes onto my plate, "there's a school group coming in later. They need wet-suit fittings. If you can do that, Weniki and I are going to get some accounting work squared away."

"No problem," I said, sinking my teeth into one of the grapes and chewing it very slowly.

"And if you get time, a new box of diving books came in and needs shelving."

"New books?" I said, lighting up. He knew I'd already read most of the diving books in my room upstairs.

"Thought you'd like that job. I wish our customers were half as keen on diving books as you and Weniki."

I glanced at Weniki, but she was so absorbed in the diving magazine, she wasn't aware we were speaking.

"I hope you're going to eat more than grapes," Uncle Tom added. Luckily, the shop's bell rang then.

Uncle Tom jumped up. Weniki reluctantly set her magazine aside and shuffled toward Uncle Tom's office. I headed for the bookshelves. As I made my way through the new box of books, I marveled at the photos of exotic fish and coral.

"I said shelve them, not read them all," Uncle Tom teased a while later. "So, you're okay with being in charge while Weniki and I do some computer work?"

"You bet!" I swept the shop and waited on a steady influx of customers all afternoon. An hour before closing, half a dozen boys my age walked in.

"Afternoon. Is Mr. McLeod in?" one addressed me.

"I'm Beverly McLeod," I said as assertively as I dared. "You must be the class that is going diving tomorrow. I'll just fetch the wet suits for you to try on."

"Excellent."

It took half an hour to fit them all. Some seemed amused that a girl their age would dare to suggest they try a size up or down. One boldly asked, "Are you diving with us tomorrow?"

I said I wasn't sure. Truth is, I go pretty stupid around guys. I'm never sure if they're flirting with me or making fun of me. I'm much better at being invisible than telling them whether their wet suits fit them. But I organized their selections into marked tubs.

"Okay. See you tomorrow, then," one of the boys said.

By the time the last one filed out, I was bushed. It was all I could do to help Uncle Tom lock up, wave good-bye to Weniki and trudge up the stairs behind him. I wanted to collapse on my bed, but I'd offered to make dinner. Dinner. That meant food. It was torturous cooking up burgers when my stomach was pinched with hunger pains. It took all my self-control to just pick at mine until Uncle Tom wasn't looking. Quickly, I hid it in the napkin in my lap, ready for the garbage.

"Want to watch a video tonight?" Uncle Tom asked.

"Yeah, sure, thanks," I said, even though I was tempted to go straight to bed.

I dozed through most of the video, but he didn't seem to mind.

"That Abe must've really worked you," he said kindly as I stood, stretched and headed for my room. "Good thing, too, 'cause I've arranged for you and a divemaster to accompany me and the school group tomorrow. Weniki can handle the shop while we're diving. I want you to have some fun while you're here."

"Thanks, Uncle Tom," I said. I wondered if I was going to be the only girl on the trip and who he'd hired as divemaster.

Chapter Four

Tanks, masks, fins, gauges, vests, weights, wet suits and booties. I checked them off as Uncle Tom called them out. Weniki and Garth helped the students load them into the van. Yes, Garth. He was the divemaster Uncle Tom had hired to help keep six fifteen-year-old boys in line.

"Are you an instructor?" a lean, blond boy asked me, eyes narrowed suspiciously.

Or maybe he wasn't suspicious. Maybe he was prepared to be impressed. I wished I knew which.

"Bev here is the dive shop owner's niece," Garth addressed my questioner. Like that made me royalty or something.

"Yeah, well I'm Bryan," the boy said, ignoring Garth and extending his hand to me with—I think—a flirtatious smile. "You going to show us how it's done, Bev?"

I shook his hand. He must have noticed mine was clammy.

"It's Beverly," I corrected him, tugging on my T-shirt hem and trying to meet his eyes. "I'm just along for the fun of it."

"Wrongo, Bev," Garth spoke up, resting a hand on my back. "I think I'll let you show all these kids how it's done."

Kids? Had he forgotten I was the same age as them? I flushed and watched Bryan's eyes shift from Garth to me.

"I have to help Weniki," I muttered as I escaped both. Imagine how Garth would be acting if this were a class of all girls, I told myself. What a player.

Somehow everyone managed to squeeze into the van, which had three rows of seats. Uncle Tom drove. Garth sat in the front passenger seat. I ended up squashed between Bryan and one of his mates in the far back.

"Been diving long?" Bryan asked me.

"A year," I said, still struggling to look him in the eye. He was pretty good-looking. "But only in lakes. And you?"

"A few months. I'm totally hooked," he said.

I nodded, and we struck up a conversation about aquatic life and the best dives we'd done. Garth swiveled around once or twice to look at me.

"You and the divemaster an item?" Bryan asked at length, leaning in close to whisper it to me. That struck me dumb for a full minute.

"Of course not." My voice sounded so hoarse, you'd think I had a cold or something.

"Didn't think so," he said with a smile, not loud enough for Garth to hear. "He's old enough to be your dad."

"*Not*," I laughed.

"So you *do* smile," he observed.

Note to self: Try not to look scared or glum when boys talk to you.

Half an hour later, we piled out at a pretty turquoise bay. Sailboats winked and seagulls soared as we unloaded and got organized. I loved the taste of the salty sea air.

"So, you're all qualified divers," Uncle Tom was saying. "Garth and I are just here to point out the sights and make sure everyone stays safe. Everyone needs to choose a dive buddy. Garth and I will do our buddy check while you're watching, to refresh everyone's memory."

Garth stood tall and ran through the exercise like a pro. I looked at the lapping water on the beach. I told myself there was nothing to be nervous about. I just wished my stomach would listen up. It didn't help, of course, that I hadn't eaten breakfast. I *had* eaten lunch, if half a papaya counts as lunch. According to that morning's bathroom scales, I'd shed two pounds so far. Only eight more to go! I knew you weren't supposed to drop more than one or two a week, but hey, I hadn't got

ter Five

k for the finger coral. And the butter-
sh. They're all over this bay. You really
en't lived until you've dived in Kauai,
v."

He insisted on calling me Bev. But it had
ring to it in his deep voice. I could get used
it. We sank beneath the surface like tourists
n a glass elevator. He made sure we went
slowly. I kept squeezing my nose to equalize
the pressure buildup, just like I was supposed

that kind of time. Ten pounds, ten days: I'm gonna do it!

The second that Garth and Uncle Tom were finished, Garth shot over to my side.

"Bev, you did fine in the pool, so I know you can do all right here. But I'll be beside you the whole time, okay? Your uncle's orders."

Uncle's orders? I wondered. But to be honest, I felt relieved. I *was* a little nervous. I always am. Knowing Garth was going to look out for me relaxed my knotted stomach.

"Thanks," I said. He winked, nodded and squeezed my arm. I turned to see Bryan look away. No point buddying up with someone who had half as much experience as me. After today I'll be fine, I told myself. As we waded into the water, I was amazed how warm it was. Winnipeg lakes can be warm, but not in the spring and fall. Next year I might get adventurous enough to go ice diving. Now *that* would impress Garth. Hey, why should I care about impressing Garth?

He's old enough to be your dad.

And

he want

reminded

But I ne

"Ready,

reached the

deflating their

pearing under the

dogs popping dow

Cha

"Loo

fly f

hav

Be

a

t

to. He made sure I did—kept watching and nodding. I felt safe with him. Soon we were thirty-five feet down. The group assembled like a school of oversized fish. With powerful flicks of his fins, Uncle Tom was circling us, soliciting the "Okay" signal from everyone.

Garth, too, was keeping his eye on the "school." As we moved forward, I relaxed my noisy breathing. Garth and Uncle Tom pointed out small, colorful damselfish and wrasses. I almost forgot to breathe when an eel slithered by. As we encountered more and more marine life, I grew giddy with excitement. Wait until I told my friends back home about this!

I couldn't get enough. I flitted here and there, lightheaded with happiness. I felt totally annoyed when someone accidentally dragged his fin along the bottom. That kicked up so much sediment that we suddenly found ourselves in a dense cloud.

Which way was up? Where was everyone? My heart thumped as I reached through the haze for Garth. I heard my breathing accelerate to a hurried gasping. My stomach tightened. Then he was there, mask against mine, hands around my waist. Even in the midst of all that swirling dirt, where not another soul was in sight, I felt calmed. He pointed his finger upward and I nodded. We rose slowly together, eyes locked, holding hands. A part of me was reluctant to reach the surface.

"You didn't panic," Garth said, releasing my hands. I heard pride in his voice. It sounded genuine.

I smiled back. "I didn't panic."

But someone had. There was a terrific splashing to the right of us. I heard Uncle Tom try and calm him down. Bryan? From Uncle Tom's concerned look, I guessed that Bryan had risen too fast, perhaps leaving his diving buddy behind. Garth left my side. He inflated Bryan's vest and spoke soothing words to him until Bryan stopped thrashing. Poor guy. A cloud of guck like that could make anyone claustrophobic.

With most of our air supply gone, we swam back toward the beach. I was so busy helping Uncle Tom load up, I never got a chance to talk to Bryan. And he definitely avoided sitting near me on the way home. When we unloaded back at the shop, he disappeared before I could seek him out.

"Hey, catch the bag of masks!" Garth called out.

I turned and put my arms out, then laughed when I saw he was joking. "Think I'd hurl your uncle's masks around like that?" he teased, moving close to me and placing a hand on my head. I glanced quickly at Uncle Tom, who seemed oblivious to Garth's clear flirtation. I did catch Weniki's frown as Uncle Tom moved inside.

"We're all unloaded," Garth said, his fingers slipping to my neck. "Take care now, Bev. No falling down any ice holes back in Manitoba."

"I'm not going home for another week," I retorted.

"Is that so?" he said, cocking his head. "Then maybe I'll be seeing you around."

His fingers rose to my cheek and lingered. Then he was gone, leaving me to rinse gear with Weniki. Her pursed lips made me realize she was upset about something. I rinsed and hung stuff until my arms ached. How did she do it all day? By the time I'd stumbled up the stairs to the apartment, Uncle Tom was cooking up a storm. But by the time his supper was on the table, I was fast asleep on the sofa. He was too kind to wake me. Another meal happily missed.

Chapter Six

As I swept the shop floor the next morning, I reflected on the previous day's dive. For sure, Bryan had been interested in me. I'd been way too slow in picking up on that. And then he'd been so embarrassed by his panic that he'd avoided me. Stupid me. I should've made more effort to talk to him afterward. I could've told him that panicking is no big deal. Wasn't I the world's expert on panicking over small things underwater?

I took his interest as my reward for losing weight. I was a whole pound less this morning already. Tired, for sure. But at least I wasn't doing anything stupid, like eating and then throwing up.

That Garth. Better be careful around him. He's way too old for me. As if he's even interested. Earth to Beverly: You're the shop owner's niece. *Be nice to the niece and get more work*. That's all there is to it.

"Beverly! How's my favorite daydreamer?" Uncle Tom popped his head over a display of merchandise. "There's a customer looking for help up front, my dear. I'm off to run an errand."

"Oh." I set the broom down and hurried over. With my level of attention today, the entire shop could be robbed under my nose.

A boy was examining the dive computers and compasses.

"Hi. Can I help you?" I asked.

"Yes, I've been looking at your instrument consoles. Can you tell me the advantages and disadvantages of a wrist-mount?" He looked me up and down curtly.

Sixteen at most, I thought. And dressed like he was made of money.

"Well," I said, "the console-mount is great, but if you're diving below 130 feet on a regular basis, you might want both a wrist-mount and console, so that one serves as a backup to the other."

The boy looked at me again, approvingly, I thought. "What about Nitrox or enriched air?"

I hesitated. "Maybe I could pull the catalog and find out for you."

"It's compatible," came a voice behind me. "So is Trimix."

I whirled around. Weniki. In my four days here, I'd hardly heard her speak two words. I knew she could speak. I'd just kind of gotten used to the fact she never did. The words came out a little funny. Sort of nasal-like. But she'd answered the boy's question.

He turned to her and began firing off new questions.

Weniki hesitated.

"You have to speak slowly. She reads lips."

"She does what?"

"She's deaf. She has to read your lips."

The boy stared at Weniki so long that I wanted to punch him. I repeated his question to Weniki. She answered promptly.

"What did she say?" the boy asked me.

I "translated" Weniki's words to him with exaggerated politeness. Her speech was clipped and tinny-sounding, but she wasn't that hard to make out.

"Does she dive?" the boy asked me in a lowered voice.

I couldn't believe his rudeness. But Weniki smiled and replied, "I dove for twenty years. I was a master instructor. I lost my hearing in a diving accident. I'd recommend the wrist-mount for you."

Five minutes later, I rang up his purchase on the cash register. The boy leaned over the counter. "Amazing, huh? That she can talk even though she can't hear? But it's not good advertising, having a diving-accident victim working in a diving shop."

I smiled to hide my gritted teeth. I didn't reply.

"Hey, so you're a diver," he continued. "That's cool. Want to go diving sometime?"

"Uh, you're welcome to sign up through our shop for a diving trip." I fished the clipboard out from under the counter.

"But would you be leading it?" he asked with a smile, leaning farther over the counter.

"Bev, need any help here?" came a voice.

"Garth!" I said with relief.

He sauntered right up behind the counter next to me. "You're interested in a dive tour, are you?" he addressed the boy coolly. "I'm the divemaster. I'd be happy to tell you where to go if Bev hasn't yet." My heart nearly stopped as he slipped an arm around my waist without losing eye contact with the boy.

"Nah, I don't need a guide," the boy said. He shifted from one foot to the other, then left the shop.

The arm slipped off my waist. I heard myself breathing again.

"So you're the shop's official divemaster now, are you?" I ventured, willing my face to regain its composure.

Garth grinned wider. "Working on it, babe."

Was he flirting with me or messing with me? Was he interested in me or making fun of me? Suddenly, I needed to know.

"Want me to put in a good word for you?" I wriggled my eyebrows suggestively. Mock flirting. Calling his bluff. Giving him a taste of his own medicine. He looked startled, for sure. But it was like trying to fake out Bobby Fischer at chess. With one swift move, he placed his hands under my armpits and lifted me up onto the counter. There, he leaned into my face.

"Dinner some night, Bev? I bet Uncle Tom hasn't had time to give you a red-carpet tour of Kauai."

If I'd had a dive tank on, the air in it would have vanished in one whoosh. If I'd been underwater, my panic attack would've scared the local fish all the way to Manitoba. But I wasn't underwater. I was sitting on the counter in my uncle's dive shop. Uncle Tom or Weniki or a customer could walk in any second. I scrambled down.

"I—I—I need to think about that," I said lamely.

"Fair enough!" he declared. "You do that, Bev. Now, I came in to drop off some papers for your uncle. I'll leave them with you and scram. Unless you need any further help with customer harassment issues." The suave grin was back.

"I'm fine," I said, smoothing my T-shirt. With a wave, he was gone.

Customer harassment issues indeed. What about divemaster harassment issues? Or had I just blown it big-time?

Chapter Seven

Uncle Tom swooped into the shop with a tray of sandwiches. "Call Weniki out from the back, will you, Beverly honey? Sandwiches are here."

"Sure, Uncle Tom," I said. "Oh, Garth dropped by with an envelope."

"Excellent. He's a good fellow. More reliable than most. I've invited him on tomorrow's boat dive."

"Boat dive?" I asked.

"Yes, I've been meaning to tell you you're invited," Uncle Tom said. "A group of instructors and divemasters is going to Sheraton Caverns."

"The place with all the lava tubes and turtles?"

"That's the one. Would you like to come along? You'll have a flock of instructors and divemasters to look after you," he said.

"I don't need a flock of anything to look after me, Uncle Tom," I said sharply.

"Of course not. I didn't mean it like that, Beverly. So you'll come along?"

"You bet. Thanks! It'll be my first boat dive."

"No kidding! Boat dives are the only way to go. Better reefs, clearer water and less swimming," he said enthusiastically.

"But Uncle Tom, I know boat dives cost a lot. Dad gave me money to cover expenses, you know…"

"Wouldn't hear of it, my dear! I'm not paying you enough as it is. Nor am I giving you enough time off. Speaking of which, Garth asked if I'd be okay with him giving you a tour of the island. Shall I tell him it's fine by me? I think it's very decent of him to offer. Sorry I haven't gotten around to it myself yet, Beverly. But you can see what this shop does to my free time."

I blanched. "Thanks, Uncle Tom. That would be nice."

"Later then, honey. I'm off. Better grab Weniki and eat while the coast is clear," he said.

I watched him hurry out the front door. Maybe Garth *was* related to Sir Gallivant. He'd actually asked my uncle permission to ask me out. Then he hadn't been able to wait. First Bryan, then the boy who bought the wrist-mount and now Garth. And I hadn't even finished losing ten pounds yet!

I found Weniki in the staff room. "Lunch is on. Uncle Tom says we'd better eat while things are quiet around here," I said when I got her attention.

We positioned ourselves so that we could see anyone coming in the door. She selected a sandwich, then lifted the tray toward me.

"No thanks. I'm really not that hungry. But those oranges look good." I reached for an orange and a knife. I could feel Weniki's eyes on me.

"Thanks for bailing me out about the compasses," I said.

I turned and saw her nod. The way she was watching me peel the orange, I had the uncomfortable feeling that she was figuring out my whole food game.

"What kind of diving did you like best?" I asked. It occurred to me that I'd never even had a conversation with Weniki before. We'd worked together nonstop for four days already. The way she was always reading the shop's diving magazines on break, you'd think it might have occurred to me before now that we had a love of diving in common. I felt ashamed of myself.

"I liked cave diving," she said, eyes turned to me.

"Really? That's dangerous," I ventured. I knew it also took a ton of training. So she'd been hard-core. "Where was your favorite place to dive?"

"Niihau."

"'The forbidden island,'" I translated. I had read about the place.

"Yes, Niihau has the most amazing sea life, Beverly. Rays, sharks, tuna…"

"You've dived with sharks?" I asked. Wow. She had my attention now.

"It's full of whitetip sharks," she said calmly. "They're magnificent creatures." As she spoke, tension seemed to melt from her face and her eyes grew bright. For a moment, I could imagine her young, strong and daring.

"Were you cave diving when your accident happened?"

The light went out of her eyes. Her face aged again. She nodded.

"You got trapped?"

There was a long silence. Then, "My husband got trapped."

Her husband? Uncle Tom had never mentioned a husband.

"I stayed with him as long as I could. Your uncle pulled me away. I ran out of air before I reached the surface."

I waited a long time, but she volunteered nothing more. I was the one nodding this time, stuck for words. Finally I said softly, "Do you miss diving?"

"I look forward, not back, Beverly. I believe in appreciating whatever health and circumstances we're given."

I reached for another orange, knife in hand. Just as fast, Weniki's hand closed around my wrist.

"What?" I said. The grip hurt, and the look in her eyes scared me for an instant.

"Eat a sandwich," she ordered.

"I told you I'm not hungry."

"And I say you will not do this to yourself," she said firmly.

Our eyes locked. Hers had a determined, commanding look.

"You're not my mother." I was defensive.

"Does your mother know?"

"Know what?" I challenged, wishing that a customer would walk in right now.

"I may be deaf, but I see."

"Well, see to your work, Weniki. And I'll see to mine," I said, voice shaking.

I walked out of the staff room. For a second, the shop seemed to spin. But I caught the edge of the sales counter and steered myself to the chair behind it.

It wasn't hard to keep myself busy the rest of the afternoon. I worked hard enough to make my uncle proud. I chose tasks that kept me on the opposite side of the shop from Weniki.

Chapter Eight

I wore a skirt and summery blouse on the boat trip. That wasn't really like me, but I loved the way the wind lifted and whipped it around my knees on deck. I loved how it made me feel feminine. I loved how slim I felt in it. I even had the start of a tan.

"Your dad said it's snowing and twenty-one below in Winnipeg," Uncle Tom reminded me. He leaned on the trawler's gunwale, a glass of orange soda in his hand. Salty spray splashed up from the boat's wake. We'd both spoken to my family that morning.

"Lucky them!" I joked, lifting a glass of diet cola to my lips.

"Maybe I can coax you back here when school finishes in the spring," he suggested. "You're the hardest worker I've ever had."

I smiled and clinked glasses with him. "But spring is when it's nice in Winnipeg!"

"Not nice like this," he said, widening his arms like an orchestra conductor.

"Not like this, for sure," I agreed. "Have I told you how much I appreciate this vacation, Uncle Tom?"

"No worries. I think it's good for Weniki to have a companion too."

I lowered my glass and studied the ocean. I felt like I'd swallowed an ice cube.

"She speaks highly of you, you know. I think she's going to miss you."

The imaginary ice cube expanded in my throat. I concentrated on the boat's wake. That's why I was the first to see the flash of black and white arch up and away from the blue.

"Look, a dolphin!" I exclaimed.

"So it is." Uncle Tom chuckled like it was an everyday event. "Try and tell me they have those in Winnipeg."

"Sure they do. They jump up out of ice holes and snatch fish from your hand, right?" Garth had sauntered over from the wheelhouse.

I giggled. He was careful not to stand too close to me with Uncle Tom there.

"And there's Sheraton Caverns," Uncle Tom said, pointing ahead. The boat slowed, and the anchor was dropped. As we geared up, two green sea turtles appeared. They seemed unfazed when we took giant strides off the boat's dive platform and sank in, neat as you please. As I bobbed to the surface, I laughed. This was fun!

We descended along the anchor line. I hesitated at the bottom as I felt a strong current.

Swim into it, Uncle Tom signaled. I kicked hard to keep near him and Garth. Soon we seemed to glide along. Lava tubes swarming with tropical fish appeared, like a movie screen dropped in our midst. I was so excited, I almost forgot to breathe. This was like all the aquatic-life posters pinned on my bedroom walls at home, come alive.

Garth had an underwater camera. He got up close to a school of blue-striped snappers. I followed timidly, afraid to be more than a foot behind him. For the better part of half an hour, that's what I did. Followed Garth like a pet dog, watched him take photos, nodded when he or Uncle Tom pointed things out. Like them, I checked my gauges regularly. But unlike them, I felt overwhelmingly tired long before it was time to turn around. At least we were swimming with the current this time.

I don't know if I looked tired or weak, but Uncle Tom and Garth started flashing me the "Okay?" signal every couple of seconds long before we reached the anchor line. And they motioned me to ascend first. I climbed it slowly. On deck I collapsed on the nearest bench, breathing hard. I felt so lightheaded.

"You go, girl!" Garth said, patting me on my back.

"Did you enjoy that?" Uncle Tom asked.

"Totally," I assured them.

"We're headed below for lunch and drinks," Garth said as everyone peeled off their wet suits. I nodded.

I even made myself eat some crackers and cheese in the salon. It was cool sitting around with a bunch of older divers, even if I wasn't allowed wine with them. Excited conversation filled the room, punctuated with easy laughter. Two of the instructors were female, but they were even older than Uncle Tom. No one to interest Garth.

"You did great," one of the instructors complimented me.

"You take after your uncle," another declared.

Garth took a seat beside me and rested his stemmed wineglass on the low table in front of us. "What can I get you?" he asked.

"I'm fine for now," I said.

"You'll need energy for the next dive," he urged.

"Hope you don't mind if I sit out the second one. I'm a little tired."

Garth looked at me closely but didn't

argue. "No problem. You can rest on the bunks below deck if you like."

"That'd be nice," I said, stifling a yawn.

"I'll show you where they are."

I let him steer me out of the room, one hand on my elbow, another holding his wineglass. Once out of the salon, he handed me the glass. "For you, madam. To celebrate your first boat dive."

Hey, why not? I took a couple of sips. In the cabin, he moved diving gear off one of the bunks and watched me lie down.

"Sleep tight, babe."

I smiled. The wine had made me feel even sleepier. It was nice and cozy in here. He leaned down. I wasn't surprised when he kissed me. It was nice. I didn't mind when he stroked my face and kissed me again. Then the hands moved down and the kissing got, well, a bit hot.

"Garth."

"Yes, babe."

"I came here to sleep."

He ignored that, was getting way too into things. I sat up, bumped my head on the bunk above, tried to push him away. He wasn't taking any hints.

"Garth!" I shouted. "Stop it!"

He was way stronger than me, but I used enough elbow power to land him on the floor. I sprang off the bunk and ran toward the salon. I was smart enough to smooth my skirt and put on a calm face before I walked in. I squeezed onto a seat beside Uncle Tom.

"Hey, Beverly. We were just talking about barracuda. Beverly reads a lot about marine life. Bet she can tell us something we don't know," he said to the group.

Barracuda, I thought. They're six feet tall, eighteen years old and have curly brown hair. I didn't say that aloud, though. "The barracuda," I indulged Uncle Tom, "is known as the 'tiger of the sea.' It's the oldest and most successful of predators."

As I spoke, Garth ambled into the salon, hair freshly combed, a smile on his face. And he winked, casual as could be.

Chapter Nine

Piles of new stock arrived the next morning at the shop, making Weniki and me super-busy pricing and putting things out on the shelves. I kept offering to do anything that required working at the back of the shop. I hoped that would help me avoid Garth if he dropped in.

Later in the morning, when Uncle Tom pulled up at the back, I practically ran to the sinks outside. "Weniki, I'm in charge of rinsing this load!"

She looked up and nodded. I was up to my elbows in water when I heard Garth greet Uncle Tom inside. I stayed out of sight. Half an hour later, when I ventured in, I wasn't sure if I was pleased or disappointed that he hadn't figured out where I was.

After serving a couple of customers, I was looking around for something to do when I noticed that it was 1:00. Uncle Tom usually picked up our lunch by now. Maybe I'd do that.

"I'm just going next door to grab sandwiches," I said.

Uncle Tom grunted without looking away from the computer. Weniki gave me a thumbs-up. Now *that* was sign language I could understand.

Next door, as I waited for our order, the aroma of food wafted around me. My nostrils were in heaven. The sights and smells tested every bit of resolve I had not to jump over the counter and scoop up handfuls of meat to shove in my mouth. Meat, bread, pickles, cookies, anything.

I could read the headlines now: "Starving girl goes mad in deli, explodes after ingesting too much."

Instead I ran a hand over my hollow belly. I was halfway to my weight-loss goal. And while I hadn't done so well in the boyfriend department yet, there seemed to be lots more lines trying to reel me in here than in Winnipeg. Maybe Hawaiian boys get *too* much fresh air and sunshine, I thought with a twisted smile.

"McLeod order ready."

"Thanks," I said, paying with my own money for once and trotting back to the shop. "Lunch is on," I announced. "I'll look after the shop while you two eat."

I perched on the stool behind the counter and willed some customers to drop in. It didn't work.

"Beverly, honey, at least come join us until someone's here," Uncle Tom insisted.

I dragged my heels into the staff room and took lots of time brewing myself a cup of coffee. I could feel Weniki's eyes on my back. I decided to throw her off my scent.

I took half a sandwich and bit into it. Half a sandwich wouldn't wreck my diet. Not if that's all I ate.

Weniki's face seemed to relax. "You finished all my rinsing," she said, her nasal voice light and her eyes kind. "What will I do all afternoon?"

I smiled. "Train me to fill tanks?"

"That's a good idea," Uncle Tom said.

"And maybe teach me some sign language," I added.

Weniki raised an eyebrow at that. Her lips edged toward a smile. Uncle Tom looked proud of me. "She's smart as a whip, Weniki. She'll have it down in no time. Not like me, right?"

Weniki laughed, her crinkled eyes taking in my uncle fondly. He saved her life a few years ago, I remembered. The day she lost her husband. Then he hired her for the shop.

"Well, I'm back to wrestling with spreadsheets," Uncle Tom announced. "Weniki, feel free to entertain my ambitious niece."

He patted me on the shoulder and headed to the office.

All afternoon, Weniki let me watch her inspect and fill the tanks, except when a customer pulled me away. It was such a noisy task that I figured deafness was an advantage. I admired her steady, sure hands. I appreciated the thorough explanations. I was sorry when 5:00 came around. Weniki had turned out to be the perfect distraction from thoughts of Garth.

Uncle Tom had left at 4:30. I'd barely locked the door behind Weniki when a soft tapping on it made me turn around.

Garth. My heart picked up, but my feet stayed planted.

"Sorry, sir, we're closed," I tried to joke. He just stood there and grinned until I opened up.

"Hey, Bev. I came around to apologize. You weren't in earlier."

Good thing he hadn't found me then. The last thing I needed was for Uncle Tom to overhear the kind of apology Garth had in mind.

I stood there stupidly, not knowing what to say.

"I forgot you were only fifteen," he said.

Now I was furious.

"I mean…" He must have seen the look on my face. "Well, I'm here to apologize. I'm here to ask for a second chance, Bev. A guy deserves a second chance, doesn't he?" He put on a puppy-dog look that would've melted anyone's heart. It was probably his most practiced facial expression. But what was I going to do, slap him or something? He'd come around to apologize. Was it so big a deal he'd gotten a bit hot? What was I, born yesterday? It's not like Winnipeg boys were always angels.

"Apology accepted," I said, trying to look stern but failing to keep the smile from surfacing.

"All right!" Garth said. "And what's happening tonight?"

"Tonight?" I thought I heard Uncle Tom's van pull up in the back. "I'm making dinner for Uncle Tom."

"And tomorrow night?"

I smiled. "I'll figure that out tomorrow."

I could see Garth's ears prick up at the sound of Uncle Tom's key in the backdoor lock. "Okay, Bev-girl. I'll check you then!" He was gone before the back door opened.

Chapter Ten

"Abe and Garth are taking a pair of divers out this afternoon," Uncle Tom announced the next morning. "If you finish filling tanks by this afternoon, you can go along."

"Thanks, Uncle Tom!" I enthused. Not because Garth was on the trip, I told myself. Just because I was getting to dive again. My time in Hawaii was almost up. And I was getting more confident each time I dived.

"The clients only just finished their certification, so you won't be doing anything challenging."

"That's okay!"

"I'm going to fill their tanks," Weniki signed to me.

"I understood that," I signed back.

She smiled. "Want to watch?" she signed.

This was fun. Like talking in a secret code. And Weniki was like a different person when she smiled.

Weniki and I worked extra hard until 1:30. Then, tired as I was, I helped Uncle Tom load the van. Abe and Garth pulled up as we were hoisting tanks.

"Hey, let us do that, Bev," Garth said, hopping out of Abe's truck and sprinting over.

I let him. I had to save my strength for the dive. Weniki appeared and signed something to me that I didn't understand.

But Uncle Tom did. "Thanks, Weniki. Beverly, bring the girls on back," Uncle Tom said.

Girls? I popped into the shop. Two lithe, native Hawaiian girls with the longest hair

I'd ever seen were chatting with each other. Sisters, I guessed. I looked at the paperwork Weniki had left on the counter for them to sign. It said they were seventeen and eighteen years old.

"Hi. I'm Beverly McLeod. You're diving with us today?" I said it like a flight attendant welcoming them aboard. Friendly but official.

"Yeah!" they said, casting long-lashed brown eyes on me and nodding.

"Come on through, then," I said. "We're all ready for you."

On the trip up, Garth was extra charming and talkative. He told us all about the bay where we'd be diving. He described the coral there in great detail. And he assured the girls he'd dived in almost every cove on Kauai.

"Which cove do you like best?" one asked, smiling and leaning toward him.

"Which cove do you live in?" he teased back.

I caught Abe rolling his eyes and grinning, as if he'd heard Garth's stories one too many times. But I had to admire how Garth was entertaining our clients. They clearly loved his stories as much as he loved telling them. He was a good divemaster, as Uncle Tom had said.

"Abe," Garth said shortly after we arrived at the dive site, "what do you think of buddying with one of the girls *and* Bev today? We're an odd-numbered group, so it has to be three and two. I'll partner with the other girl." He was looking at the older sister. She was standing in her bikini, changing into her diving gear. Her long hair danced in the breeze.

He knows I've been diving enough this week that I don't need special attention, I told myself. They're the paying clients, after all.

We suited up, waded in and submerged. It was nice diving in such a small group. Abe and Garth were quick to point out eagle rays and lionfish. They were also very attentive to the girls. I thought the sisters looked pretty confident considering they'd only just been certified. But then, they'd grown up around here. They'd probably snorkeled all their lives.

We took a break after forty minutes in the water and returned to the beach. Garth gave me money to fetch some drinks and snacks from a nearby shop. When I returned, everyone was relaxing on the beach, catching some rays, laughing and talking.

"So," Garth was saying loudly, "inside the underwater wreck, I was just heading toward the door when this pack of hammerhead sharks swam past a porthole."

"Whoa," the older sister said, eyes big, as she rubbed suntan oil in circles around her navel.

"What'd you do?" the younger sister asked.

"Well, I grabbed my camera and started photographing them. But the flash caught their attention and they slowed down to check me out."

"Oh no!" the sisters chorused.

"I had to hide in a cubbyhole onboard until they were gone," Garth said.

"But he lived to tell the tale," Abe finished, sitting up to accept the drink I set down beside him.

"Hey, thanks, Bev," Garth said, glancing up.

Our second dive was shorter, and I got a little bored. But the girls seemed pretty psyched, judging by how much they talked about it all the way back to the shop. Actually, I don't know if they chattered all the way back, because I fell asleep on the rear seat. I was glad I'd had the doze, however. Because after we'd sorted out all the gear and said good-bye to the girls, Garth sauntered back into the shop.

"So, Miss Winnipeg. Do I finally get to show you around Kauai tonight, starting with dinner?" Good thing Uncle Tom was out just then, the way Garth leaned really close to me and ran a hand through my hair.

I could smell the salt and suntan lotion on his shoulders. I kind of wished he'd kiss me again, right there. But then I caught movement out of the corner of my eye. When I pulled away and looked, there was no one, but I guessed it had been Weniki.

"Sure," I said. "But let me wash up and meet you there."

He named a restaurant a few blocks away. He named the time.

"See you, Bev-girl," he said, winking as he left the shop.

I showered and came downstairs in my favorite summer dress and some heeled sandals. It was 5:30. I was surprised to see Weniki still there.

"I'm off to the library," I lied. "I left a note for Uncle Tom."

She nodded. But her face had none of that morning's friendliness.

Chapter Eleven

"You look stunning out of a wet suit," Garth exclaimed as I neared the restaurant's door. He looked dashing in a silk shirt.

"Your feet are much shorter out of fins," I tossed back.

"And you smell nice," he said, leaning close to me and sniffing.

"Are all Hawaiian guys as smooth as you?" I asked.

"Not a chance," he replied, holding the door open with a porpoise-sized smirk.

A maitre d' guided us to a linen-covered table near the stage, where a four-piece band was set up. I'd never been to a place like this in my life. I noticed right away that most women here were way better dressed than me. I felt a bead of sweat form on my forehead.

"A half carafe of the house red," Garth said to the waiter when he came around.

The waiter turned his eyes to me.

"Do you and the lady have ID?"

Garth lowered the wine list and raised an eyebrow in mock amazement. "The lady and I do not have ID. Do we need ID? Seriously?"

The waiter fidgeted as he studied Garth. "Perhaps not, sir. A half carafe of the house red."

I could hardly believe it. The waiter was giving us a break? That Garth and his charm.

He grinned and propped up a menu for us to share. I gazed at it and found the words swimming in front of me. After a near-full day of work, two dives and some sunbathing, I was running on empty. The few minutes' sleep in the van had done nothing for me after all.

I tried harder to focus. And I realized, to my horror, that he was planning to pay big money for food I couldn't eat. After nearly a week of starvation, I couldn't face food. The very thought was making my stomach writhe. Of course it was all in my head. But that's how things stood. So what was I doing in a restaurant for dinner where the entrees cost more than Garth made on several dives? What was I thinking when I'd agreed to this?

I reached for my glass of water. The buzz of conversation around the cavernous restaurant was making a vein pound in my forehead.

"I'm thinking the steak and prawns," Garth was saying. He waited politely.

"I'll start with the celery-pecan salad," I said, tightening my jaw to prevent a yawn.

"And then?"

"Can I just stick with that for now?" I hoped I didn't sound like I was pleading.

"You're saving yourself for dessert, I can tell," he teased.

We clinked our wineglasses together. Against my better judgment, I took a few sips. He ordered our food as the band struck up a tune.

"Do girls from Manitoba dance?" Garth asked, taking my hand in his.

I got the sense I didn't have a choice. I let him pull me onto the dance floor. His body swayed comfortably to the beat. His smile encouraged me. But unused to wearing heels, and seriously tired, I tottered uncertainly.

When a heel buckled under me, he was quick to catch me. He pulled me into his arms as the music slowed. This was easier. I let him steer me in slow motion. I leaned into him for support. Was that glitter on the walls, or were my eyes doing something strange? I looked at the ceiling, tables and band members. They all had stars on them. Black stars. As Garth spun me unexpectedly, I nearly sank to the floor. He caught me and pulled me up.

"Bev, are you okay?"

"A little dizzy or something."

"Do you get dizzy often?" That was his first-aid training speaking. He was a good divemaster, I thought hazily.

"I have the edge of a migraine."

"Oh."

"I think—we should—maybe sit down. I'm sorry."

"It's okay," he said, but I knew he was disappointed. All dressed up and a dud for a dance mate.

It wasn't the wine, I thought as I watched our table spin toward us. It couldn't be, so soon. The salad might help. I sank into my chair and studied my lap. It was the only place that didn't have black stars.

After a while, I dared to look up. Garth was staring at me.

"Your face is sheet-white," he said quietly. "Are you sure you're okay?"

I nodded and reached for my glass of water. I was thirsty, so very thirsty. I took big gulps and realized too late that I'd picked up my wineglass. I felt the wine snake into my shrunken, shaky stomach. I might as well have dropped a match into an empty gas tank. I forced a smile at Garth as an internal battle erupted.

Our food arrived. My unsteady hand brought a forkful of celery and pecans to my mouth. I forced my lips to part. The food sped toward the battle, but it was too late.

"Please excuse me for a moment," I mumbled as I stood up and headed for the ladies room.

How I made it there, I don't know. I think someone helped me. It had to have been a lady, because I ended up holding onto her all the way into the toilet stall. When I emerged—I'm not sure how long after—an aproned waitress had replaced her. And Garth was standing right outside the ladies room to take over from her. I don't know if he got to eat any of his steak and prawns. My memory is a bit blurry about some things, but I know he added a taxi bill to the evening's expenses to get me home. And Uncle Tom came into it somehow. He and Garth were on either side of me as I floated up the apartment stairs. I think I remembered to say "sorry" a couple of times.

Did Garth remember to tell Uncle Tom that we'd been at the library? Had I told Garth we were supposed to have been at the library? Possibly our breath didn't smell like we'd been at the library.

That was not a successful date, I thought to myself as my head hit the pillow. I hardly heard Garth's and Uncle Tom's whispers outside my door before I sank into a deep sleep.

Chapter Twelve

I woke up late, but Uncle Tom wasn't down-stairs. He was at the breakfast table, waiting for me. He poured me a bowl of cereal. He placed it in front of me. After a minute of looking at it, I realized he was standing over me like a guard. So I ate some spoonfuls. What else could I do?

"I get migraines sometimes," I said. "I'm really sorry I was trouble last night."

Uncle Tom cleared his throat. "I wish I'd known that. Do you have some medication you can take for them?"

"Yeah."

It's true that I get migraines. Not often, but now and again. Usually a simple old aspirin and a nap do the trick. Never have my migraines decorated walls with black stars before. But if Uncle Tom didn't buy it, I was in a truckload of trouble.

"Guess I'd better call Garth and thank him today," I said.

"You're darned lucky he's a responsible young man."

Ha! I thought. But I nodded and met my uncle's eyes. "I am."

"When he asked if he could show you around Kauai, it never occurred to me it would be a dating sort of situation. Not with the age difference between you two."

I dipped my spoon into my cereal, not trusting myself to look at him.

"So can I assume there's nothing of that sort going on here?"

"Yes, Uncle Tom."

"Even though you were not at the library?" His voice had risen in volume.

My spoon stirred the cereal. "I wasn't sure you'd let me go to dinner with him before he toured me around. I was afraid you'd think it was something it wasn't."

Uncle Tom's fingers drummed the breakfast table. Being a bachelor, he wasn't very good at this role. I smiled and touched his hand. "I'm sorry about last night, Uncle Tom. I don't get migraines very often. And it's totally gone now. I'm fine."

His fingers stopped drumming. His face softened. He stood up.

"Sorry I got suspicious, Beverly. I trust you, my dear. Now, tomorrow is Christmas Day. Garth has offered to take you diving at Koloa Landing. Are you feeling well enough for that? I'm going to come along if I can break away. But if I can't, we'll have Christmas dinner when you return. I've invited Weniki over. She doesn't have family."

He smiled. "Besides, she's a heck of a cook, so it lessens your chances of having undercooked turkey and overcooked Brussels sprouts."

I smiled. "That's awesome, Uncle Tom. I look forward to it." I hadn't weighed myself that morning, but I was guessing I was down another pound or two. So I could afford to eat some Christmas dinner. I wouldn't spoil things for them by not eating.

Chapter Thirteen

"Weniki says this is Kauai's best dive site," I said, leaning out of the cab of Garth's pickup truck to let the wind toss my hair.

Garth lowered his mirrored sunglasses and glanced sideways at me. "Weniki is a wise woman. And you look like an excited girl."

"She did say to be careful," I said, popping my head back in.

"That's why you chose the best dive-master on the island." His arm shot over to pull me closer.

"And the most modest." I punched him lightly. "Weniki and I filled the tanks together. She's training me to be a 'tank jockey.'"

Garth laughed. "No kidding. You aiming to take over your uncle's shop?"

"You never know. If I do, I'll increase your hours to whatever you like."

"Ooooh, I'd better keep on your good side then," he crowed as he parked near the launching ramp. He leapt out and flung open the back of the truck. We pulled the gear out and suited up in record time. Buddy check done, we towed our buoy a quarter of a mile to where the coral reef dropped off.

"Ready, Bev-girl?"

"Ready, Garth-boy."

We had sixty minutes' worth of air, but Garth seemed to be in a hurry. I pumped my fins as fast as I could, but I could tell I was holding him back. I'm way out of shape, I thought. My breath was coming hard. I was exhausted and relieved when he finally slowed. He turned and flashed the "Okay?" sign.

"I'm okay," I signaled back. He checked his gauge, then checked mine twice, as if surprised by how much I'd depleted my air supply already. As we propelled ourselves along the reef, stunning coral formations grabbed my attention. Large schools of fish swam right past our masks. I paused to check out a gallery of shrimp, some resting in holes in the coral. I had an urge to crawl in and rest myself.

Time passed quickly. When Garth signaled "up," I returned the "okay" signal. He set the pace. It was nice and slow. Good thing. I felt so spent that I could see black stars when I closed my eyes. The idea of blacking out underwater scared me. I'd better eat something before our next dive, I thought.

By the time we'd surfaced and swum to an unpopulated stretch of the shore, I had nothing left in me. I crawled above the tideline and collapsed. Garth helped me out of my wet suit and laid out a beach towel.

"Rest, babe," he said.

I rested. I might even have dozed in the warm sun. I awoke to a trickle of water running down my neck. I opened my eyes.

Garth was stretched out beside me, grinning, a water bottle in his hand.

"The divemaster says you need to rehydrate. Open your mouth."

I smiled and propped myself up on one elbow to accept the water. A dribble ran down my chin. He caught it on a fingertip, then played the finger around my lips. He pulled me toward him, started kissing me. I wasn't really awake yet. I'd have liked some more water. I felt thirsty, weak, disoriented.

His hands were caressing, slower than last time.

"Bev-girl."

I wanted to tell him to leave me alone, let me sleep. I reached one hand out for the water bottle. He intercepted it and placed it on his chest. I fought a little, then thought, who cares? Didn't I make a vow to lose ten pounds and catch a guy? Haven't I done both? I lay like a rag doll.

But things got out of hand really fast. I came to my senses and used whatever strength I could muster to roll out from under and crawl away. I crawled toward the truck, which shimmered like a mirage in the noon sun. I aimed to pull myself into it and lock the door.

I glanced back. I saw him plunge his fist into the sand, but he didn't follow me. I didn't make it to the truck. I just lay on my stomach, wishing the water bottle were near. Wishing I'd never agreed to come diving here. Wishing I hadn't lied to Uncle Tom. And knowing I needed food.

Chapter Fourteen

I guess I drifted off to sleep again. I woke up to the smell of chocolate. Garth was waving a chocolate bar under my nose like it was smelling salts. I sat up.

"I think you need to eat something," he said, eyes narrowed. "And drink." He shoved a bottle of power drink at me. I struggled up and took that eagerly. I drained it.

I picked up the chocolate bar and bit into it. Unbelievable. The chocolate swirled around my mouth, igniting all my taste buds. I closed my eyes and licked my lips. I felt revived. I felt wonderful. I felt ready to dance to the beat of the waves lapping near our feet. I looked at Garth, wondering if he was mad at me. He was polishing off a sandwich, eyes on my face. He grinned.

"So, I've unburied your secret at last. Chocolate is all it takes." He jumped up and fetched our second tanks from the truck. "Well, we've driven way too far today to settle for one dive, Bev. Ready to suit up?"

I thought about protesting, but I didn't. I had a vague sense of owing him something. So I took one more bite of the chocolate bar, drank some water and joined him.

He didn't hurry me on the swim to the buoy. The sun beat down, little whitecaps splashed our faces, and the reef beckoned. It was a perfect day. I was doing okay for energy. Better, anyway.

Ten minutes later, we were moving along the sandy bottom at forty feet when Garth tapped my shoulder. I followed his pointed finger to a white-spotted toby. It looks like it has measles, I thought as I surveyed its spots, big eyes and stubby nose.

Garth was inspecting every wall cavity we passed. At one hollow, he flicked his fins excitedly and beckoned. As I came near, he gripped my hand and pulled me closer. I brushed against the reef and felt something loosen around my waist.

I looked down. My stupid weight belt. I hadn't fastened it tightly enough. It was slipping down. I worried it might come off. I began fiddling with it. I felt his hands encircle my hips, pull me toward him. I pushed him away. *Not now*, Garth.

The hands came back. This time I felt angry. He couldn't seem to control himself, even under water. I lifted the clasp on my weight-belt buckle and tried to cinch up the strap. But just then, Garth bumped against me. I lost my grip and the belt slipped down to my thighs. I also lost my temper. I pushed the inflation button on my buoyancy vest to give me a quick lift away from him. At the same time, I kicked him, hard. An instant later, I felt my weight belt slip to my knees.

I reached down but missed grabbing it before it fell away.

Uh-oh. With no weight belt, I was headed for the surface. I grabbed for the valve on my buoyancy vest to deflate it. At least I remembered that would help slow me down. I was going up way too fast. I kept working the valve on my vest and exhaling. I knew I had to exhale to keep the air in my lungs from expanding too fast.

I kept expecting Garth's hands to grab my fins and yank me back. But hadn't I just kicked him? Maybe he was mad. Or maybe he couldn't catch up with me. Without my weights, I couldn't reverse direction and check on Garth.

The pressure changes were inflating my vest faster than I could deflate it. My body tingled with fright, but I wasn't panicking. I knew I was doing everything I could. I looked down. I could see Garth now, ascending with hands raised. He was coming up fast, in a cloud of bubbles. I looked up. The dark blue water was fading to white where the sun penetrated.

When I came to the surface, I gasped some fresh air, then plunged my head back into the water to look for Garth. He shot up beside me: mask off, eyes closed. His regulator was out of his mouth. Blood was running from his wet hair down his forehead, below a bump. His vest was puffed up.

"Garth!" I screamed.

I grabbed him by his shoulders and shook him. His eyes stayed closed. My heart cartwheeled. Unconscious. No. Please not.

I tried to inflate his vest, like I knew I was supposed to. That's when I realized it was already fully inflated. No wonder he was floating so high beside me. He's a divemaster, I thought. He knows better than to let his vest inflate that far on the way up. He should have been deflating it to help slow his ascent. With trembling fingers, I inflated mine so that I could keep a good grip on him. Then I grabbed the whistle on my vest and blew like a crazy woman. Some divers on the launch ramp looked my way. I waved my arms wildly, a distress signal. Two who'd not yet put on their tanks hurriedly donned fins and snorkels. They pushed off and swam toward me.

I pulled my mask down around my neck and tilted my cheek over Garth's mouth. I could feel no breath. Heart pounding, I cupped the bottom of his head in one hand and pulled myself up enough to give him three quick breaths.

He responded by coughing and spluttering.

Relief flooded me. "Garth!" I shouted. He wasn't responding, but he was breathing again. As my helpers neared, I racked my brain for what else I'd learned in divers' training.

Jettison his gear for faster towing. When I went to release the weight-belt buckle, I realized it wasn't there. He'd dropped his weight belt to get to the surface faster. To chase me? To save himself?

The first helper reached me. "Unconscious but breathing," I reported. "I don't have the strength to tow him." Damn my stupid diet, and lucky for me that they were around.

The diver nodded. He double-checked Garth's breathing and pulse. Then, keeping

Garth face-up, he collared the back of Garth's vest. Splaying his own feet and arms out to either side of Garth, he kicked and stroked to tow the victim's body backward toward shore.

It was a towing position I'd practiced many times with my Manitoba diving friends. It had always been a fun exercise. But nothing was fun about watching this diver pull Garth's limp body.

"Are you okay?" the other diver asked me.

"Yes," I said, but the true answer was "weak."

My chest heaved with the strain of returning to shore. I wished a hundred times on the way that I'd been eating sensibly the past week. I wished a hundred times that I hadn't kicked Garth.

I wondered what I'd done to make this happen. He was a divemaster. He knew how to recover from anything. But as I swam, I put it all together. My kick must have dislodged his mask and regulator at the same time. My weight belt must have landed on his head. Stunned and searching blindly for his regulator, he'd ingested water. His divemaster instincts made him attempt an emergency ascent. That's why he'd risked dropping his weight belt and fully inflating his vest. He'd hoped it would carry him to the surface before he lost consciousness. It almost had.

The divers on shore were gathered around Garth. "We don't have a phone," one told me. "Do you?" I found the strength to sprint to Garth's truck. I rummaged through his stuff until I found his cell phone. I dialed the emergency number.

Chapter Fifteen

I remember the ambulance arriving. I remember the police car taking me home. I remember Weniki and Uncle Tom coaxing the whole story from me. And I can still recall Weniki feeding me some turkey and cranberry sauce before putting me to bed. But mostly I remember the dream that took over as soon as my head sank into my pillow.

I was wearing a fur coat. That's stupid, because I don't own a fur coat, and I never would. But I was wearing a fur coat and running barefoot around an ice hole on a lake in Manitoba. My breath was coming in terrified gasps. I clutched the coat around me because all I had on underneath was a bikini. I knew I didn't look good in the bikini, and I was afraid of my coat flying open and exposing my flab and white skin.

I was circling the hole at high speed, with Garth chasing close behind. I was sure he was trying to push me into the dark circle of water. He was shouting something, but my ragged breath drowned it out. He was gaining on me. Then I heard him.

"Get away from the edge of that hole!"

I paused for a second. That's when he grabbed me and dragged me away from it. I stood there shivering and confused, my bare feet numb. Garth stared at me. Not at my face, but at my coat. His hands moved to open it. His eyes locked on my bikini. He shook his head as if disappointed. My shivering increased. I wanted to cry.

But when he spoke, it wasn't what I expected.

"Bev," he said, eyes sad, "you're not eating enough. I'm disappointed in you. You can't dive looking like this. It's not safe."

He released his hold on my coat, which fell back to hide my body. I turned to look at the ice hole. I felt a force rise from it, reaching out to me, pulling and sucking me toward it.

I flung my arms out to Garth. He clutched me by my hips. He was trying to help me, but the force was stronger. As it ripped me from his clutches, he collapsed on the ice, unconscious. I started screaming.

Uncle Tom and Weniki heard me and came slipping and sliding across the lake. As I looked at Garth's still body, anger replaced my panic. I dug my fingers into the ice and clawed away from the hole. Summoning all my strength, I resisted the pull until Uncle Tom and Weniki reached me. They halted my slide toward the hole. I crawled back to Garth.

"Garth! Garth!" I shouted.

Weniki's hand was on my forehead. I opened my eyes.

"You're having a nightmare," she said.

I looked around my bedroom. Uncle Tom was beside her. No light leaked from under the window curtain. It was the middle of the night.

"I was having a nightmare," I confirmed.

Weniki lifted my water glass to my lips.

"How's Garth?" I ventured.

"You saved his life by keeping your cool, Beverly," Uncle Tom said, "though you and I need to talk about your diet and your lying, and Garth is going to have to account for some of his behavior." He paused to let that sink in, then reached for my hand. "Diving-wise, you did everything textbook-right yesterday. I'm proud of you. He's going to be okay."

Everything right? Not true, I knew. When his hands had gripped my hips underwater, he'd been trying to help me with my weight belt. I knew that now. He hadn't been hitting on me underwater. He hadn't deserved a kick. I'd almost killed him.

Chapter Sixteen

Eggs, blueberry pancakes and bacon sat heavily in my stomach as I made my way down the hospital corridor toward Garth's room. But I'd relished every last calorie of them this morning. Of course, Uncle Tom had hung around to make sure I did.

The door was ajar. I hesitated before I knocked.

"Bev," he said with a lopsided grin. He was propped up, reading a diving magazine.

A small bandage graced the top of his forehead. Half a dozen vases of flowers decorated the nightstand on the far side. A box of chocolates beside them was nearly empty.

"Do I start with an apology or a thank-you?" His face looked slightly sheepish. "If I certify you as an honorary divemaster for saving my life, and I admit that I probably deserved that kick—although maybe not the timing of it—can we still be dive buddies?"

He reached for my hand.

I sat down on the chair beside the bed, but kept my hand to myself. "Garth, it was very stupid of me. I thought…"

"Of course you thought. Hey, didn't I say I kind of deserved it…?" His eyes looked genuinely contrite.

"But I never imagined…"

"Even divemasters have soft heads! Remember that now that you're an honorary divemaster, Bev-girl."

I tried to smile as I met his eyes.

"Accidents happen," he continued. "What matters is how well you responded. Bev, you saved my life. I'm thanking you, okay?" His hand reached out and lifted mine from my lap. "The rest is"—he paused and smirked—"water under the sea."

"Good thing those other divers were around."

"Yeah, good thing given how Popeye's Olive hadn't been eating her spinach lately. At least that's what your uncle was explaining to me on the phone this morning. I should've clued in way before yesterday. What were you thinking, Beverly McLeod, mixing starvation with diving?"

I smiled weakly. "Learned my lesson, Divemaster."

"And maybe or maybe not, I've learned one too," he said ruefully, squeezing my hand before releasing it. "Hey, you think we'll get written up in one of the diving magazines?" He lifted his glossy and waved it at me. "Best stuff is always the dramatic near-deaths and how they coped. Don't you agree?"

"Not sure we need to divulge all the details of how it came about."

"I'm glad we agree on that," he said with a wink. Then his face grew more serious.

"Guess I've lost an important source of dive-master gigs."

"Don't count on it. Uncle Tom has lots of dives with no female clients."

Garth smiled and mimed yanking a dagger from his chest. "Now, if I'd had half a notion when I first met you that you were so capable of taking control when a situation calls for it—I mean, you can really kick ass when you're taking control…"

I giggled despite myself.

"…I'd have asked you out way sooner."

"Sure you would've."

He produced an exaggerated sigh. A rap on the door made us look up.

"Lunch, Mr. Olsen." A pretty girl in a Candy Striper uniform, maybe seventeen years old, entered with a tray in one hand and a bunch of flowers in the other. She nodded brightly at me as she set them down. "More flowers arrived too. You seem to be the most popular patient on this floor."

"Absolutely, and don't you forget it. Not to mention totally available to help you with arranging my flowers later," he replied with a wink. Then he caught himself. "Oh, Laurel, meet my girlfriend, Bev. Bev, this is Laurel, the friendliest Candy Striper employed by this lovely establishment."

"The most tolerant, anyway," Laurel said with a smile and wink at me. "You've certainly got yourself a charmer!"

"Laurel," Garth said, "do me a favor and bring a second tray for Bev? She's starving."

"Sure, I can do that," Laurel said before I could protest.

Garth winked. "See? I come recommended by a Candy Striper. Does that mean you'll give me another chance?"

I raised an eyebrow as my tray appeared. "Sunfish don't swim with barracudas," I pronounced. "And I fly home to Manitoba tomorrow."

He nodded gravely. "Have lots of boyfriends back there?"

I was too busy tucking away my lunch to reply immediately. When I'd polished off everything on my tray, I said, "I've decided that I need boyfriends like you need another weight belt on your head."

Garth's hand went up to touch his bandage. "Still, it's a unique souvenir, and we might get written up."

I grimaced, then stood slowly. "Well, it's been real, Garth Olsen. Thanks for being my best dive buddy in Kauai." I said it solemnly. I meant it.

"You'll be back, Bev. And I still owe you an island tour. But if I get an urge before then to go ice diving, can I look you up?"

I laughed. "Please do." I leaned over to plant a kiss on his forehead. His hand came up to pull me down for a kiss on the lips. That was okay by me. Then I turned to go but had one more piece of business.

My fingers glided across his bed to the chocolate box on the nightstand.

"Take two, Miss Winnipeg," he said, and I did.

Pam Withers is author of *Camp Wild, Raging River, Peak Survival, Adrenalin Ride* and *Skater Stuntboys*. She is also a former summer-camp coordinator, whitewater kayak instructor and river raft guide. She lives in Vancouver with her husband and teenage son when not touring North America giving school presentations. Her website is www.TakeItToTheXtreme.com.

OTHER TITLES IN THE
ORCA SOUNDINGS SERIES

More Orca Soundings

Home Invasion
by Monique Polak

I was turning the corner to my street when I spotted the key. Someone had left it right in the lock of their front door. I walked up the front stairs and raised my finger to the doorbell. My plan was to let whoever lived there know they'd forgotten the key.

I didn't ring the doorbell. I turned the doorknob and let myself in.

Josh is less than thrilled that he has a new step-father and finds his personal habits—and his personality—irritating. Resenting his new living arrangements and his unorthodox home life, Josh finds himself drawn to the idea of a "regular" family and, on a whim, sneaks into a neighbor's house to see how others live. Considering it a harmless pastime, Josh continues entering people's houses until he is witness to a violent home invasion. Josh must use all his courage to save himself and bring the home invader to justice.

More Orca Soundings

Snitch
by Norah McClintock

The cop pulled a photograph out of his pocket.

"You recognize this, Josh?"

"Those are your initials, aren't they, Josh?" the woman cop said.

I nodded.

"It's what Scott was hit with. We have it down at the police station, Josh. Besides your initials, it has your fingerprints on it."

Josh had been living in a group home after being ratted out by Scott, his one-time best friend. Now he has moved in with his brother and overbearing sister-in-law and has been sent to a class designed to teach him to deal with his anger. When an old enemy continues to push his buttons and Scott appears to be up to his old tricks, Josh struggles to control his temper. Framed for a crime he didn't commit, it will take all of his newfound strength to keep his cool—and his freedom.

More Orca Soundings

Yellow Line
by Sylvia Olsen

Where I come from, kids are divided into two groups. White kids on one side; Indians, or First Nations, on the other. Sides of the room, sides of the field, the smoking pit, the hallway, the washrooms; you name it. We're on one side, and they're on the other. They live on one side of the Forks River bridge, and we live on the other side. They hang out in their village, and we hang out in ours.

Vince lives in a small town—a town that is divided right down the middle. Indians on one side, whites on the other. The unspoken rule has been there as long as Vince remembers, and no one challenges it. But when Vince's friend Sherry starts seeing an Indian boy, Vince is outraged and determined to fight back—until he notices Raedawn, a girl from the reserve. Trying to balance his community's prejudices with his shifting alliances, Vince is forced to take a stand and see where his heart will lead him.